Liberty A
and the
Terrible Scare

Written by Kat McMann
Illustrated by Zoe McMann

To order additional copies of this book, contact:
Xlibris
1-888-795-4274
www.Xlibris.com
Orders@Xlibris.com

ISBN: Softcover   978-1-9845-8431-1
        EBook   978-1-9845-8430-4

Print information available on the last page

Rev. date: 06/19/2020

Liberty Acres

and the

Terrible Scare

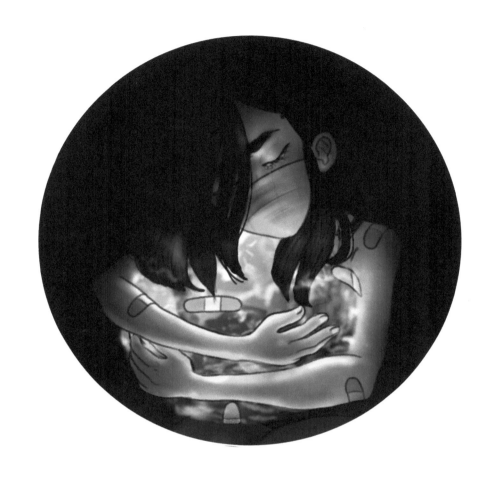

We dedicate this book to
the frontline workers and first responders
for their courage and dedication
during the
Coronavirus pandemic.

- Kat and Zoe -

On Liberty Acres Farm all was well.
Winter was ending the critters could tell.

They were joyous with the coming of spring
and for the wonderful things spring would bring.

Then, one day, a hush fell over the land;
a strange silence they could not understand.

No one knew why there was no one in sight
or why the family had tucked in tight.

So Vi, the chickadee, said she'd fly out
to learn what was happening all about

and come back, quick as she could, with the scoop
so they all could be kept in the news loop.

Waiting anxiously for the news they'd get,
they all hummed, as the sun began to set.

When, at last, Vi returned she didn't feel well
but perched on a limb and began to tell.

She gave her report with a sad-toned song
and, to their dismay, they learned before long

that a dreadful dust, blowing through the air,
was covering everything everywhere.

It was a horrid thing, this dust, it was
and this dust scared everyone just because

they hadn't seen anything like this before
and so, that scared everyone even more.

Some folks were caring for ones who fell sick
while others were trying to find the right fix.

When Vi was done they knew
what they should do.
They would have to get, safely,
tucked in too.

Libby Lou Ladybug flew to her nest.
Moe Mouse scurried back home, as it seemed best.

Tate Cat and Jax Dog stayed on the front porch but could still chat with others back and forth.

Clancy Pig and Grady Goat kept from harm
by sheltering up, safely, in the barn.

Katie Cow and Rosie Horse
joined them there.
To keep themselves and
others safe, was fair.

Staying put was I, Mighty Mama Oak,
with my little acorns tucked in my cloak.

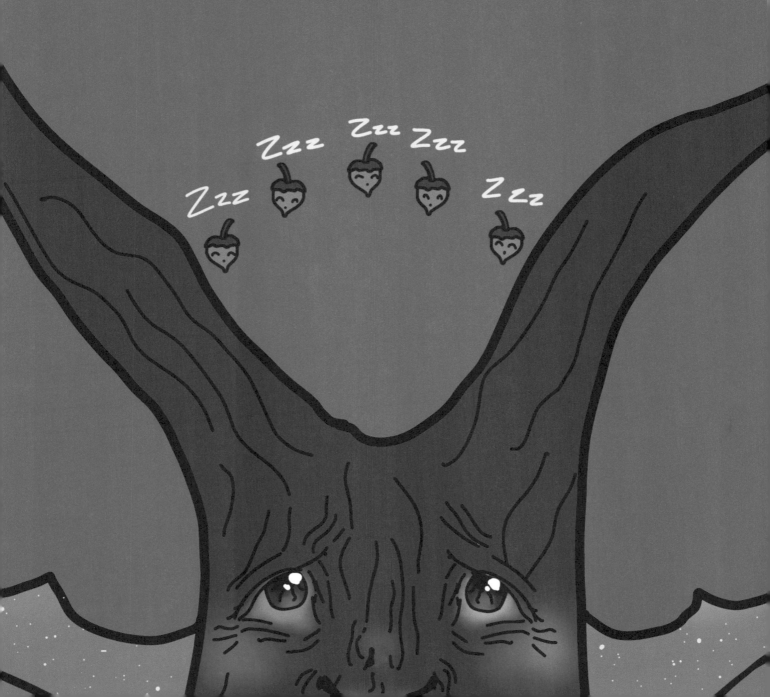

Baby Nut Nuts, and his squirrel kin
there too,
caring for Vi who seemed to have
the flu.

Then, though
the stillness,
came sounds
from afar.

Uniting,
in song,
under a
bright star.

Together, by the light of the full moon,
they made a wish for all to be right soon.

We are not sure what the next day will bring.
In the meantime, let's continue to sing.

Sing praises for the workers everywhere
sacrificing so much because they care.

Sing praises to neighbors, strangers and friends,
with their show of love a breaking heart mends.

Sing praises to families holding strong.
Home is our heart's beat and where we belong.

Sing praises to all trying to keep us calm
while giving advice to keep us from harm.

Sing songs together of faith, hope and love.
Make a wish upon a bright star above.

We're all in this together,
that is true,
and with faith, hope and love
we'll make it though.

- Kat McMann

CPSIA information can be obtained
at www.ICGtesting.com
Printed in the USA
BVHW021205020720
582815BV00003B/29